MW00893772

felipe
the flamingo

Jill Ker Conway

Illustrated by Lokken Millis

FULCRUM PUBLISHING
GOLDEN, COLORADO

Library of Congress Cataloging-in-Publication Data

Conway, Jill K., 1934-
Felipe the flamingo / written by Jill Ker Conway ; illustrated by Lokken Millis.
p. cm.
Summary: Felipe is small for a flamingo of his age, and his feathers and legs are not pink, but with the help of some friends he sorts out his problems and begins to feel better about himself.
ISBN 1-55591-547-7 (pbk.)
[1. Flamingos—Fiction. 2. Growth—Fiction.] I. Millis, Lokken, ill. II. Title.
PZ7.C7686Fe 2006
[Fic]—dc22

2006002636

ISBN-13: 978-1-55591-547-6
ISBN-10: 1-55591-547-7

Printed in China by P. Chan & Edward, Inc.
0 9 8 7 6 5 4 3 2 1

Fulcrum Publishing
16100 Table Mountain Parkway, Suite 300
Golden, Colorado 80403
(800) 992-2908 (303) 277-1623
www.fulcrumbooks.com

felipe the flamingo

lived in a salt marsh on a beautiful coral island with his mother and father, two aunts and two uncles, and five cousins.

Felipe's parents worried about him a lot because he was very small for his age and hadn't yet turned the deep rose pink color that makes flamingos so beautiful. Sometimes his aunts and uncles laughed about him, and his tough, older cousins teased him and called him "The Albino."

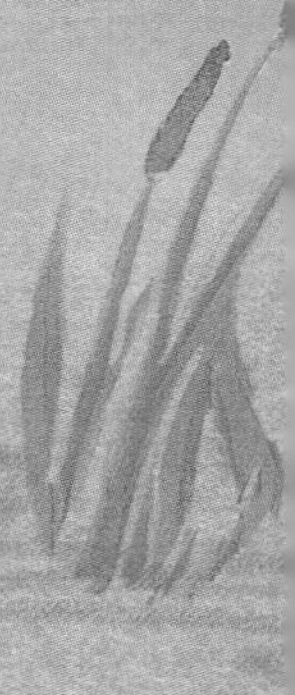

Felipe couldn't help being small and pale. His neck was too stiff to reach down to the marsh's mud floor and feed all day on the shrimp and little crustaceans that lived there. He could only manage to eat for a few minutes at a time, so he didn't eat enough to grow fast like his big cousins. And he never ate enough of the pink shells that give flamingos their color.

Felipe also couldn't sleep well because he couldn't tuck his head back under his wing the way the other flamingos did to go to sleep. His neck was just too stiff to bend back that far.

Felipe's mother was the kind of person who acts cross when she's really worried. "Felipe," she'd say sternly, "you're just lazy and won't try." But then, when no one was looking, she'd slip him a beak full of shrimp under the cover of her wing.

Felipe's father was a much gentler person and tried to hide his worries. "Felipe, son, don't worry. You'll grow out of that stiff neck. Just try your best. Eat as much as you can. I know you are going to grow pink and tall."

One day, Felipe noticed that his mother and father kept going off together and talking a lot. They weren't eating, either. They paced about as though they were arguing. Felipe wished he could hide his eyes under his wing because he didn't like seeing them argue, but he caught glimpses of them looking very upset.

Eventually, at sunset, they came to stand beside him. Trembling a bit and sounding a little cross, his mother said, "Felipe, this marsh is eaten out. There isn't enough food here for the whole flock. We have to fly two islands away to the south, where there is a very big marsh with lots of food."

Felipe felt terrible and looked away to where the sun was turning the clouds pink as it set. He knew he still couldn't fly very far. He just wasn't like his cousins, who kept taking off and flying around with their long pink legs sticking far out behind them.

His father kept a wing around him while his mother said, "You know your father and I are the lead birds for our flock. We show everyone the way, and they follow us." She choked a bit, and then said firmly, "So we have to go." But almost before she'd finished, his father said, "It won't be too bad. I'll be back in four days. Then I'll stay with you till you are big enough for the flight."

Felipe was suddenly very frightened. Before he could say, "You mean I'll be ALL ALONE," his mother said quickly, "I've talked to my friend Eleanor Egret, who won't be leaving this marsh. She'll keep an eye on you and stay near you at night."

Felipe looked across the marsh to where Eleanor Egret was stalking fish. With her white feathers, bright yellow legs, and beak showing against the dusk, and her wild, spiky head feathers making her look a little crazy, he didn't feel she'd be much help if he was lonely.

His father suddenly flew away, and then, just at dark, he came back with a beak full of shrimp for Felipe. Then they both tried to rest.

The next day, at first light, when there was a hint of silver near the line of the ocean and the dark clouds to the north began to reflect the light, Felipe's father took him over to the island where Eleanor Egret had her nest. "Goodness, he is small," she said tactlessly.

Then, trying to be comforting, Eleanor Egret said, "Well, Felipe, maybe I can teach you to fish."

His father gave him a gentle brush with his wing and said softly, "Remember, I'll be back. Be sure to wait right here for me," and then very slowly he went back to the flock.

Felipe shook all over with grief as he watched his father and mother lead the flamingos away. He was sure he would never see them again. Then, after they grew tinier and tinier in the sky and he couldn't see them anymore, he stuck his head under his wing as far as he could and cried.

All of a sudden, it was bright sunlight. Eleanor Egret was off fishing, and Felipe was huddled down in the water crying. Then, just beside him, from one of the bushes on the marsh island came the most beautiful song. He looked up to see a bird with black wings, a white breast tinted pink, and long black tail feathers with white tips. It was Monique the Mockingbird, who sang so beautifully to him that he stopped crying and began to feel a bit better.

"What's the matter?" she asked. "Why all the tears? And why didn't you go with the other flamingos? And why aren't you even a little bit pink?"

Felipe told Monique about his very sore neck, which he just couldn't bend down to feed on the marsh bottom, so he didn't get enough food and was too weak to fly long distances. He began to feel very sad again as he thought about his mother and father.

"Don't cry anymore," Monique said kindly. "The water in this marsh is already very salty, and it doesn't need you to put lots more in with so many tears. I'm going to fly around the island and see if anyone knows of a flamingo with a stiff neck and what to do to cure it. I'm sure someone will know. We'll get it better before your father comes back, and maybe then you can eat enough to be pink when he sees you." With that, she gave a few more trills and then flew away so fast she was just a black speck in the sky in seconds.

Eleanor Egret came rushing back with one shrimp in her beak for Felipe. "Heavens, the child's thin," she said. "How will I ever feed him enough so he doesn't fade away?" Then she was gone again.

Felipe knew she meant well, but her wild eyes and spiky head feathers made him think of a ghost, and he thought she was the most tactless bird he had ever met.

Around noon, Monique was back, trilling excitedly. "There was another flamingo with a stiff neck once, over at Turtle Cove, on the other side of the island. He was cured by stretching his neck on a turtle's shell in the hot sun at midday. So I asked Terence the Turtle to come and try it with you. He'll be here tomorrow morning so we can all be ready when the sun gets hot. You'll see. We'll get you better." And then she flew off.

Felipe felt better already, just thinking about stretching his neck. But he was hungry. He suddenly realized he had had only one shrimp all morning.

Just as he was making some tries at getting his neck down to the bottom of the marsh, he heard someone paddling. He looked up to see a small fair-haired girl in a yellow kayak staring at him. He stared right back. He saw that she had grey eyes, and her hair was plaited in a long pigtail down her back.

"Hello. What's the matter? Can't you bend your neck? Want me to push to help you?"

"No," said Felipe firmly. "It's too stiff. I can't bend it, but I keep trying because I'm hungry for shrimp."

The girl, who said her name was Gloria, sat looking at him from her yellow kayak. "I know what," she said. "I'll go home, go to the supermarket, buy some shrimp, and then bring them back to you."

Felipe wasn't sure what a supermarket was, but he said politely that he thought it would be nice to have some shrimp. So Gloria turned her kayak around and was gone, paddling as fast as she could go.

At first, Gloria's mother and father couldn't understand why she wanted to go to the island supermarket to spend her pocket money on shrimp. They thought her story about the stiff-necked flamingo was funny, until she got out her bicycle and said she would ride there in the heat of the day, it was so important. Then her mother said she would drive her and wait outside while Gloria bought a pound of shrimp and would then help her mash it up in a food grinder so a small flamingo could eat it.

Gloria went inside, but it was the first time she'd been inside the big supermarket by herself. She ran around everywhere looking for shrimp, but she couldn't find any. She thought about Felipe waiting for the shrimp, and her eyes began to fill with tears.

"What's the matter, young lady?" a very tall attendant asked her. "Have you lost your mother?"

"No," Gloria said crossly. "She's waiting for me outside. But I can't find the shrimp, and I need some fast for a friend."

The tall attendant smiled and told her to follow him. When they got to the freezer where the shrimp were, there were lots of packets of different sizes.

"How much do you want?" her new friend asked.

"How much should I get for two days for a very small flamingo?" she asked.

"For who?" he said. So Gloria told him all about Felipe and why she wanted the shrimp right away. He thought for a while. "He'll eat the shells and all, won't he?" he asked. "Better take a pound in case he's *very* hungry. That should do it. Come with me and I'll get you out fast." With that, he walked right up to a vacant cash register and rang up her total.

By two o'clock, Gloria was back with a big pail full of shrimp that she held just at water level so Felipe could eat them with saltwater to wash them down. He was *so* hungry, he emptied the pail before he knew it. It felt very good to feel the food sliding down his throat. To thank Gloria, he stood tall, flapped his wings and bowed, and told her he felt much, much better.

"I'll bring some more tomorrow," she said. "But then our island holiday is over, and I have to go back home." She started telling Felipe about her home in New Jersey when Monique came by. They all discussed how to get more shrimp for Felipe until his neck was better.

"I know," said Monique. "We'll have to find Pete the Pelican. He's a bit rowdy, and sometimes swears like a sailor, but he's got a kind heart and a big bill. He could bring you shrimp. They say there are still quite a lot on the other side of the island."

So Gloria and Monique set off to find Pete, and Felipe enjoyed not being hungry. He even tried flapping his wings and flying a little, until Eleanor Egret, who was fishing on the other side of the marsh, called out not to go too far away.

Then, before he knew it, Felipe saw that it was dusk. Tonight his tummy was so full, he felt drowsy, so even though he couldn't get his wing right over his eyes, he fell asleep right away.

The next morning, Monique woke him up with a cascade of triumphant trills. "Terence the Turtle will be along very soon, and I found Pete the Pelican late yesterday. He'll be over tonight with some shrimp. Just eat it, and don't ask too many questions, or he'll start boasting about his adventures at sea, and you won't be able to get him to stop."

Just then, Eleanor Egret raced up with one shrimp in her beak, gave it to Felipe, and turned nervously to Monique to ask how she thought Felipe looked. "Why, he's looking fine, and by the time we've stretched his neck today, he'll look even better."

Eleanor looked suspicious. "Who's doing that? I'm supposed to keep an eye on him. What will his parents say if his neck gets too long?"

“Terence the Turtle is coming, and Felipe will stretch his neck on his shell,” Monique said. “His neck won’t get too long. He’ll just be able to bend it.”

Eleanor Egret looked uncertain. “I have to begin fishing now over by that island. Call me when this turtle, who I don’t know, arrives.” And with two flaps of her wings, she was gone.

After she was out of sight, Monique got the giggles, which she disguised as a lot of pretty trills. “Felipe,” she laughed, “do you think Eleanor Egret ever has fun?”

Felipe thought about it carefully because, for all her nervous ways, he’d come to like Eleanor. “I think she’s lonely,” he said, “and has no one to laugh with.”

Just then, there was a sudden ripple in the water, and there was Terence the Turtle. He was bigger than any turtle Felipe had ever seen. He had four thick flippers, a long neck, a small head, and wise eyes. Felipe thanked him for coming.

“Not at all,” said Terence. “I remember having a sore neck once. It must have been eighty years ago, when I was very young, but I can still remember how nice it was when it got better. Now let’s get down to business. The sun is over there on our right, so you must stand on my left side and

bend over as far as you can toward my right side. Make sure to tuck your beak under the edge of my shell. Then hold on with your wings. I'll pull away a little to stretch your neck, and then we'll just let the sun warm it for an hour or so."

Felipe did as he was told. Monique flew around offering advice. "More to the left, Terence. Felipe, hold on tight." And they swam around slowly in the sun with Felipe beginning to feel a knot he only dimly understood start to untangle in his shoulders.

Satisfied that her plan was working, Monique flew away to tell Eleanor not to worry and to see if she could make her laugh.

While he lay there dreaming great dreams about growing strong and turning a deep rose pink, Felipe saw two orange fritillaries land beside him on Terence's shell. The butterflies had soft, silvery voices, so he had to listen hard to hear them.

"Felipe, we watched you flapping your wings to fly yesterday, but you had a hard time getting going. Just watch us for a minute and see how we move our wings gently and steadily from the center of our backs. That's the way to move once you get in the air," one said. Then they both lifted up and circled slowly around in formation so he could watch them up close.

After they had done three or four circuits of Terence's shell, Felipe thanked them and said he'd try to copy them just as soon as he was finished lying on Terence's back.

Suddenly, they were gone. The sun was so warm, Felipe felt drowsy. And there he was, very comfortable, when Gloria appeared in the yellow kayak with lunch. She looked hard at Terence and Felipe, and then laughed. "I can see now what Monique meant about stretching Felipe's neck. It must feel lovely."

Terence popped his head farther out of his shell and said they'd done enough for one morning. He was going to snooze over by Eleanor Egret's island, where the water was a bit deeper.

Felipe flapped his wings and stood upright beside the yellow kayak. Gloria's pail was even fuller than the day before. This time, Felipe minded his manners, ate slowly, and stopped to talk to Gloria from time to time. Did she mind going home to New Jersey? Did she have brothers and sisters? What was the supermarket like, and how did they come to have so many shrimp?

They didn't get past talking about how much Gloria hated going home because, all of a sudden, she nearly dropped the pail. "Felipe," she almost shouted, "I think you are turning just a little bit pink. Wait till Monique comes back and sees this! If Pete the Pelican just does what we asked, you'll get pinker every day. Then no one can tease you."

Felipe couldn't quite believe her, but she was so insistent, he began to imagine what he'd look like with his white feathers all pink and his legs a nice rose color. She told him she had two brothers back home who teased her a lot, and he told her all about his five cousins and how he hated it when they laughed at him.

"Well, they won't the next time they see you," Gloria said happily. "If Pete does his work right, you'll be just the same color as them."

Then they talked about saying good-bye because Gloria had to go home. She said she'd come back once more, later in the afternoon, after she'd packed, just to see how the stretching was working and whether Pete had brought shrimp. And they agreed that they'd look out for one another by going to Eleanor Egret's island when Gloria came back next winter.

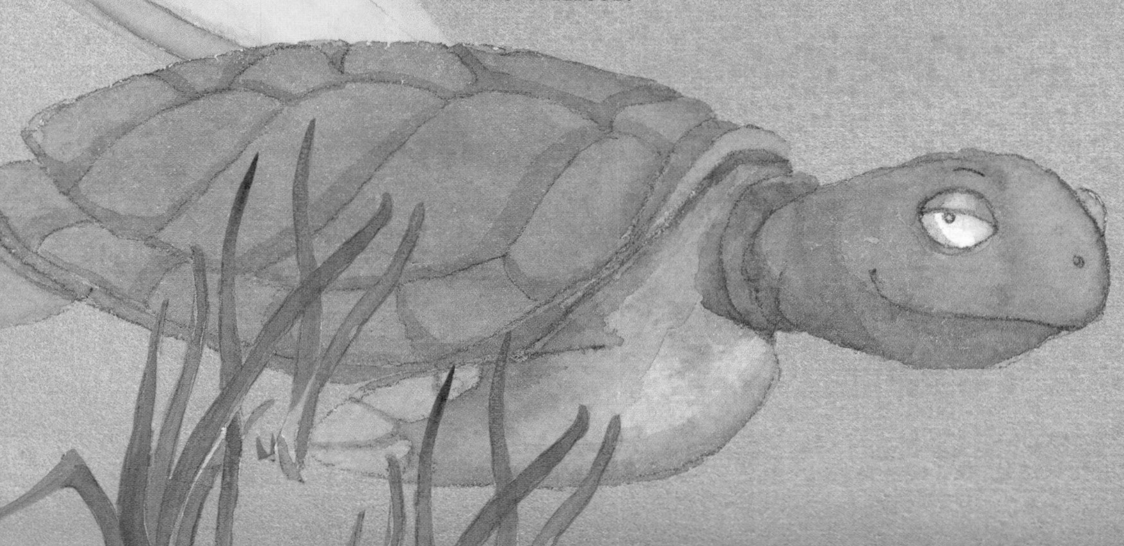

As she paddled away, Terence came sailing majestically back and said cheerfully, "Alright, Felipe. Now we'll really get down to business. Lie right down on my back, let your legs hang out behind you, and tuck your beak under my shell, right by my neck, and then just hang on tight. We're going to go as fast as I can. But don't worry, you're loosened up now, and your neck should stretch easily."

So Felipe did as he was told, and they raced away, up the marsh and back again, so fast that Felipe's neck was stretched to its full length. "Now," said Terence very casually, "just pop your head under your wing for me."

And without thinking about it, Felipe tucked it in almost all the way.

That was just the way Monique found them when she flew back to see how everything was going.

Terence was very proud, Monique was excited, and Felipe almost couldn't believe what was happening.

Monique had come to announce that Pete would be arriving with a big bill full of shrimp, so Terence went off to snooze in the afternoon sun, and Monique went to visit Eleanor and tell her the good news about Felipe's neck and his new pink color.

When Pete came, Felipe could see why Monique called him a bit rough. His grey feathers went every which way, one of his eyes had a scar under it, and he looked ready to laugh at the world and handle any danger that came his way.

He sat on a rock low to the water and opened his bill, which was enormous and full of all kinds of little shellfish.

Felipe had to put his head inside the bill to start eating, but he settled down to an excellent meal.

Pete had never fed a flamingo before, and he wasn't prepared for how Felipe's beak would

tickle the inside of his mouth and make him want to laugh. He tried hard not to and concentrated on thinking about soaring over the sea and getting ready to drop right out of the sky to catch just the right fish. But at last, the tickling feeling made him sneeze an enormous sneeze that made all of the remaining food in his bill splatter all over Felipe.

"Bejasus!" he shouted. "Sorry, old sport. Couldn't help it. Your beak was tickling me."

Felipe couldn't help laughing, and Pete began to laugh too, a big, raucous laugh that sounded very jolly.

"Next time, I'll drop all the shellfish on Eleanor's island. There's a little hollow rock there that will do just fine to hold them. I'll be back." He flapped his huge wings and was gone, his loud laughter echoing across the marsh.

Felipe set to work cleaning himself, grooming the feathers on his chest, under his wings, and around his neck. Suddenly, he stopped and stood absolutely still.

He'd pulled out a feather that now floated in the water just beneath his eyes. He could see that it was pink, and then he believed he was really better.

So he flapped his wings and then began to fly, using his muscles just the way the fritillaries had told him, and he found Monique.

"Monique, I'm turning pink," he shouted, "and look how I can fly."

She began to fly around him, trilling,

"You're turning pink,

turning pink,

pink,

pink,

PINK!"

Soon they were back at Eleanor Egret's island, where Terence popped his head out from inside his shell. Eleanor flew back, and Pete arrived and dropped his shrimp so he could sing bass to Monique's trilling. Then Terence began to beat time with his flippers, and Eleanor, who turned out to have a lovely voice, began to harmonize. And Gloria, who'd come sadly to say good-bye, began to beat time on the side of the yellow kayak, and the two orange fritillaries floated down to sit on the side of the kayak.

"Felipe's turning pink,

he's turning pink, yes,

he's pink, pink,

pink,

PINK!"

They made so much noise that they woke up Benedict the Bahamian Owl, who lived in a cave over on the next headland, who flew over to watch what was going on.

Felipe had never seen an owl before, so he landed right beneath the mangrove branch so he could see the owl's big, wise face better.

Then everyone began telling Benedict the Owl Felipe's story. And then Eleanor Egret got straight to the point. "Benedict. You are so wise. Why did Felipe get that sore neck, and will he stay better now?

Everyone became quiet and began to listen. Felipe thought Benedict had a voice as beautiful as his big, big eyes, and he listened so intently, he was hardly breathing.

"Well, Felipe, I think you may have had growing pains. Lots of creatures get growing pains just as they start a growth spurt. But yours lasted so long, your neck stiffened up. But you see, it's nothing to worry about. Look how Monique and Gloria and Terence and Eleanor and Pete took care of you."

They were all so intent on listening to Benedict that they scarcely noticed that the sun was setting and the half-moon was beginning to glow brighter along with the evening star. And no one noticed the black outline of a bird flying toward the marsh, which grew bigger and bigger and then turned rose colored, until finally, Felipe's father settled down in the water right by Eleanor's island.

"Eleanor! Where's Felipe? You said you'd watch him. Where is he? He's not lost, is he? Did he try to follow us?

When we got to the south island, I just couldn't stop to rest. I just had to get back. But *where* is he?"

"Why," said Eleanor proudly, "he's right there. Hasn't he grown? And look how pink he is."

So then they had to tell the story to Felipe's father, and Felipe took off and flew slowly around to show how he could fly. Then he landed right beside his father, put his head right down to the mud in the marsh, and then brought it up and tucked it right under his wing, just to show his father that the whole story was true.

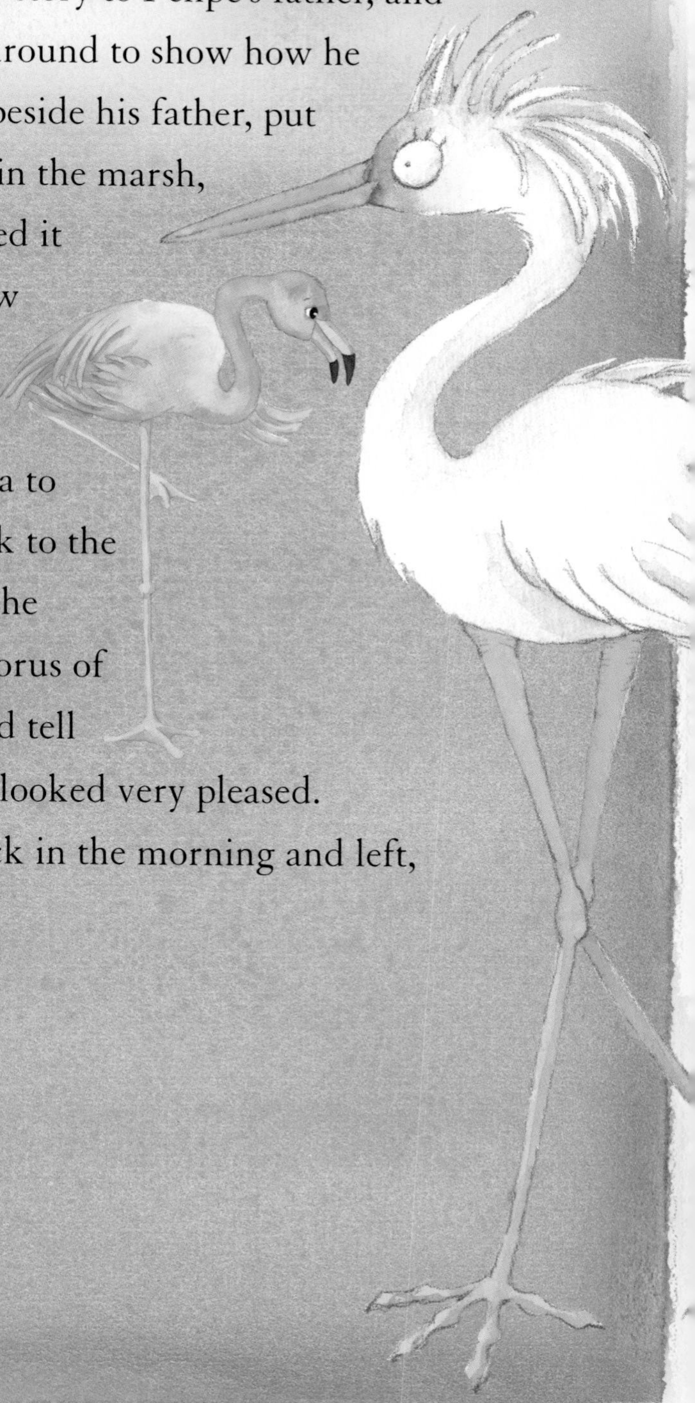

Then it was time for Gloria to go home, promising to come back to the very same place next winter. So she paddled off slowly to a whole chorus of good-byes. Pete said he'd stay and tell some sea stories to Eleanor, who looked very pleased. Monique told Felipe she'd be back in the morning and left, still trilling,

"Felipe's turning PINK,

he's very PINK,

PINK,

PINK!"

Benedict the Owl reminded Felipe never to worry about growing pains again and then said it was time he went hunting. The butterflies left to rest on some sea grape flowers, and Terence set out for Turtle Cove, saying how happy he was that his help wouldn't be needed anymore. And Felipe and his father ate some of Pete's shrimp before they settled down to rest.

Early next morning, they needed to fly around the island to thank everyone again and then leave quickly for the island in the south, where they knew Felipe's mother was waiting and worrying. As he fell asleep, Felipe kept thinking how wise Benedict was, how happy he was to be a real flamingo color, and what fun it would be if his teasing cousins didn't recognize him.

When they set off the next morning, Felipe's father looked back at the island and said, "Felipe, you are pink now, just like all the other flamingos, but you will always be different too because you have had such a great adventure here."

And Felipe knew it was true.